MW00596686

This book is dedicated to everyone who ever told me that it was ok to follow my dreams, no matter how crazy they may seem :)

<u>Introduction</u>

Hello Reader! Thank you for choosing to pick this book up, it truly means a lot to me, the author, and to those who have lived through this story. The core of this book is based on a true story. The real people who lived through the events of this book have decided not to reveal who they are. Which is why I have taken the liberty of changing characters, locations, and company names. When I found out about this story, I instantly knew that the world deserved to hear about it. I hope you enjoy this book as much as I enjoyed writing. The greatest compliment an author can receive is a book recommendation to friend of family member. Thank you so much!!

Chapter 1

Watching the sun rise slowly over the ridge and reflect its growing presence across the lake, I slowly rocked in my chair and sipped on my steaming coffee. From inside the house, I heard Kaitlyn coming down the stairs and outside. She kissed my forehead and sat on my lap wrapping her arms around my neck. We sat in silence for what seemed like forever to not disrupt the earth's daily routine. The wind gently played with her blonde curls and the newborn rays of sunlight brought out the color of her eyes; that's an ocean I don't mind being lost in. My heart swelled with pride as I wrapped my arms tighter around her.

When the sun reached the tops of the great oaks just past the fence line, she looked at me and said, "You've got a plane to catch.," she then walked back in the house and began cooking breakfast.

I slowly rose from my chair and walked down the driveway to the barn and grabbed a couple of flakes of alfalfa. As I walked toward the gate, all three of our horses raised their heads in curiosity. In excited anticipation, they began to walk towards their respective stalls to await breakfast. They ate slowly and deliberately, without a care in the world. If only my life could move this slowly. From the time I was fifteen years old, I was an independent, free-willed mustang. No force on earth could tame me. I wanted better for myself, I was tired of being treated like I was trash, and by God, I achieved better. At the age of twenty-one, my net worth was nearly 5 million dollars; however, I was diagnosed with a pituitary gland tumor. The surgery went well until I had an allergic reaction to a pain killer. This sent me into cardiac arrest. It was the worst feeling in the world to be in so much pain yet still be completely and utterly helpless. If it wasn't for the quick response from the nurses I would have suffered extreme brain trauma and I would have never been the same.

Today is the two-month mark on my journey to complete recovery. I could not be more blessed, Kaitlyn spent every night in the hospital with me, making sure I was taken care of. Even when I was released, she made sure I didn't overextend or re-injure myself. She was everything I had ever prayed for. She was a blessing sent right from heaven and she embodied every aspect of the perfect woman. I do tend to be quite 'bull-headed' and I'm not a fan of having people help me. But when I was released, there were a lot of things I could not do on my own, no matter how hard I tried. I couldn't get dressed without getting light-headed, I couldn't get in an out of the shower because the pain was so immense, and the fact that she was willing to be there for me truly opened my mind to the fact that sometimes help isn't a bad thing.

Today is also the day I'm traveling to Nebraska to attend the wedding of my close cousin's and to take care of some farm affairs. A few years ago, when my great uncle passed, he divided the family farm up between every family member that was legally able to own land. A lot of family members decided it wasn't worth keeping their land because they would never visit the farm again. The remaining few who wanted to keep their sections began to buy out other family members. I ended up falling into this category, and by the time dust settled, I owned the second largest chunk spanning an impressive 4500 acres. However, the unintended side effect of my uncle's generosity was that legally anything that happened to the farm had to be decided with everyone's approval. This means that any changes to the land, any large financial expenditures, and even down to which crops to grow had to be voted on by everyone. For a while this was not an issue, the farm cranked out so much money in soybeans and corn that each of us started spending a chunk of the money on ourselves. My cousin

Robyn bought herself a new car, I'm using some of the money to pay for my college, and my cousins that have a decent chunk of the farm, use the money to pay for their daughter to be in club sports. Other family members just enjoy visiting and spending time in the place they grew up. The first decision all of us made was to hire a farm manager. Since very few of us actually lived near the farm and the rest were too busy running the family's aluminum trailer company, Starlight Trailers, having someone else run the farm seemed like the easiest thing to do. The man we hired was Rucker Davis, a personal friend of Archer's. I don't know many details about him but for the past two years he seems to be doing a good job, and he seems to be making us more money every year.

My head hit the wall of the airplane as the wheels and tarmac collided, waking me from my short nap. The short flight from Dallas to Omaha was supposed to be a designated time to get some work done, however, my brain and body screamed for rest. As I stepped out of the airport, I felt the cool breeze brush against my face. The heels on my boots knocked against the concrete, turning heads. Wherever I traveled to in the United States or even around the world, it was clear I wore my Texan heritage with pride. Dressed to the nines in boots, starched jeans, button-down shirt, and cowboy hat I was sure to turn heads wherever I went. I made my way to the rental facility, the sun peaked out from behind the clouds. A small headache formed as I approached the counter, this was my least favorite part of traveling. I despised the rental car process for some unknown reason, maybe it's the fact that these companies have found a way make money on an item that depreciates so rapidly, it just seems like cheating the system. I finished the paperwork and exchanged that for a set of keys. As tempting as it was to splurge for the truck or SUV, I knew that I had a truck already waiting for me at the farm, so I ended up with a Nissan Versa. It was quite the show to see me get in and out of this thing, it was exactly like watching clowns pile out of a tiny car.

The two-hour drive from the airport to the farm was quite a scenic one. To a normal person, one might see miles and miles of corn, the occasional pig farm, maybe a few cows and horses here and there, they would see enormous silos and tiny towns with a single gas station and old fashioned diner. Once outside of the micro-metropolitan area of Omaha this is the scene anyone can easily spot.

However whenever I drive, I see the farmer who has plowed his acres with pride, I see the family in the run-down house who hopes this year's soybean harvest will provide the much-needed facelift to the house, I see the families who have sold their soul to the mega-corporations to prevent foreclosure, I see the many families who are balancing bank loans, battling mother nature, leveraging their land, but most importantly the families who wake up every day, despite those adversities, with a smile on their face because they have to the best job in the world.

Chapter 2

The pavement turned into gravel as I neared the farm. My right foot pressed firmly down on the accelerator as the dust cloud trailing me grew. My anticipation was growing, and I was ready for a pee break too. The blue sky was as clear as could be, the sun radiated down and reflected off the waxy corn stalks. I rolled down the windows and the cool breeze blew in as my worries blew out the window. As soon as I came over the hill, I could immediately see the bright red barn and three small silos, I could see the long blue barn and the remains of an overgrown feedlot. I was finally home. Throughout my childhood, I would periodically visit this place for a family reunion, wedding, or funeral. My fascination with the place never ceased, as a kid the farm was a place for my imagination to run wild, as an adult the farm was a place of escape and relaxation.

As I pulled into the gravel driveway, the entire family rushed out to greet me. Everyone laughed and got back to work getting things ready for the big day tomorrow. I went into the old farmhouse and grabbed my truck keys off the wall rack where they had been neatly hanging until my return. Looking around very few things had changed. The old oak dining room table and the matching kitchen cabinets, the navy-blue carpet my aunt had wanted just after she got pregnant for the third time, the wallpaper that filled the walls had an old elegance that could never be replaced. The new appliances and some new furniture gave the place an added character. The wall of pictures that had more and more filling it stared at me as I glanced over each and every one. There were pictures of almost every family member present on the wall, in the last few months of my Uncles life, it was these pictures that gave him relief. The picture that caught my eye was a picture from my high school graduation, oh how I've changed from that chunky kid who was bullied for most of his childhood.

I grabbed my cousin Archer so we could talk and drive. The green grass around the house had reached a healthy state after the harsh winter. When we got to the barn, I was dwarfed by the sheer size of it. If the panels could talk, they would share stories of the different phases the farm has gone through over the years.

When my grandpa was living here, the farm was used to produce enough food for the family to survive, and by listening to the stories, I have found that often times the farm produced more than enough food for a large family living in the early 1900s. Then when my Uncle inherited it, the farm transitioned to a monoculture state by raising dairy cattle, then pigs, and finally a very successful beef cattle feedlot. The flaking paint and stress marks on the wood showed the barn's age. I yanked on the slow creaking barn doors to reveal a flatbed Ford dually that hadn't seen the daylight since I had last visited. The door creaked open and a fine layer of dust coated the inside and out. With one deep breath, I cleared the dust away. I slid the key into the ignition and the old diesel engine roared to life.

Driving around the farm, I always choose to see firsthand the health of the crop and the land. This small break also allows me to catch up on issues that might need resolving. The rows of corn were enthralling, watching them as you drive by was extremely satisfying to the mind. I rolled down all the windows and turned the radio down.

"Alright Archer lay it on me," I said

"We are out of money," Archer said hesitantly.

My heart sank and a million thoughts raced through my head, but I took a deep breath and calmly, "How are we out of money."

"I don't know, everything on paper is normal. I looked at all the records in the house, and even did some math and everything checks out."

I did a quick turn from the pasture to the road. My gears were grinding and the tension in my head began to build. I pointed the truck towards town and leaned on the accelerator. The lines on the highway started going by faster and faster. I glanced over at Archer, who was sickly pale with fear, and said,

"There has to be something you're missing. We're going to the bank so I can see every transaction on paper, hopefully, we can figure this out."

In just a few minutes, I aggressively pulled into the first parking spot available at the bank. I flung the door open and power walked to the front desk with Archer trailing behind like a puppy. The bank teller looked at me with concern, and asked, "What can I do for you today?

I quickly replied with, "I need every bank statement available for the past five years."

The color from the bank tellers face drained quickly at the notion of my request, "Five years?"

"Yes!" I said confidently.

He clicked on his computer for a minute before replying, "It'll take a little bit to gather all those records, you can have a seat in our waiting area, and we will bring them out when we are finished."

I nodded and went to take a seat in the waiting area. Archer kept staring at me, not saying a word for a solid five minutes before finally breaking, "What are you doing?"

"It's simple really," I replied, "We need to figure out our problem, so I need to see every transaction before and after the farm was divided up. This could shed some light as to why we are suddenly out of money."

"But how can you verify those transactions? How can you be sure they're accurate?"

"I'm not looking to verify the transactions; I'm looking for outliers. Meaning that somewhere in those documents there's something that doesn't add up." I fiddled with the table full of magazines and finally decided on *Forbes*.

"That's why you're the businessperson," Archer said.

It wasn't long before the bank teller came over with a box full of papers and said, "Here you go sir, these are all the transactions to happen on your account for the past five years."

"Thank you and have a good day," I replied with a smile. He looked at me like I was insane. Maybe I was.

Chapter 3

Trying to hide the fact that I spent all night invested in those bank statements, I adjusted my bowtie and wiped my forehead with a wet paper towel. I strolled out of the bathroom and took a glass of champagne off a waiter's tray. The glass felt dainty and fragile in my hands as I walked to my table, locking eyes with family, friends, and even people I didn't know. The wedding was quaint, but the reception was grand, with no spared expense. I took a seat waiting for the bride and groom to enter.

I spied something peculiar from across the room. My young cousin Lexi was rearranging the name tags on some of the tables before taking her own and walking over to my table.

"What are you doing young lady?" I asked her.

She replied, "I'm moving tables, I can't stand being with all the kids."

"Out-growing the kids' table at age fifteen already?"

"Yep, Uncle Marvin can sit there now, and I get to sit next to you."

I couldn't help by chuckle a little, "What if I wanted to sit by Uncle Marvin and listen to him drone on about his brand-new yacht or his European vacations?"

Lexi rolled her eyes and smiled as she went to replace the name tag. When she came back, she sat down next to me and I leaned over and said, "Don't grow up too fast on me."

I'm not quite sure when it began, but somehow Lexi and I became close. It was unexpected, like a rainbow at the end of a storm. Since her parents refuse to be just that, it seems to have fallen on the backs of everyone else in the family to guide this delicate angel in life. For some reason or another, I am one of the few adults she listens to and respects, and that has given me more of an incentive to be a good role model for her. I deeply care for her like the little sister I never had. If you were to ask her, I'm confident she would agree.

"How's school?" I asked her.

She hesitated for a second, "It's going well."

"What do your grades look like?"

"Um…they're not bad."

"What's not bad?" I questioned.

"I mean I have a perfect score in band and health."

"What about the important classes?"

"They're all almost B's"

"Lexi," I said in a disappointing tone.

"What?!" She replied, "It's not my fault they're all terrible teachers."

"That's an awful excuse," I rolled my eyes, "what have I always told you about that."

She sighed, "You always say I'm responsible for my own learning."

"And?"

"And that if I don't understand something, I need to do anything in my power to learn it because knowledge is power, power is money, and money means I can go shopping at the mall."

"Exactly," I said, trying to be serious, "When's your next band concert?"

She brightened up and said, "It's in two weeks on Friday."

"Hm, well I guess Kaitlyn and I are going to have to come."

Lexi had a mix of emotions ranging from shocked to ecstatic, "Really?! Y'all would do that!?"

"Of course, we wouldn't miss it for the world."

Lexi jumped up and hugged me tight and I hugged her back.

The night continued with an expensive steak dinner, and I indulged myself in plenty of booze which clouded my thoughts from the impending doom I had to deal with tomorrow. The reception concluded with dancing, which at this point, I had plenty of alcohol in me to let loose. In normal instances, I would enjoy a nice two-step or line dance, however, when alcohol was added into the mix, my dancing seemed to get a little more provocative. The strobe lights danced around the room and played tricks on my mind. When I finally got back to the farm I passed out from sheer exhaustion. But my mind continued to work all night long.

The smell of Folgers being brewed is enough to wake anyone out of a slumber. I lumbered downstairs to find a lot of the family members who have stakes in the family farm were up enjoying breakfast. My cousin Leena fixed me a nice plate of biscuits and gravy, then I took my seat at the table. Once everyone got settled the questions started pouring in. All of them concerned about us not having any money.

I spoke up, "I looked at all the bank statements and there's no unusual activity until I can figure out what happened we need to figure out what to do to get some money in the bank quickly."

Everyone seemed to agree with that statement. We all sat in silence for a few minutes, eating our breakfast. Leena piped up first, "What if we sell all that hay out in the barn, that'll be some quick capital."

"That's a good start," I said, "Any other ideas?"

Archer replied, "the local high school doesn't have a place to keep their stock show animals since the barn burned down, what if we converted the old barn on the south end of the property to a place where we can rent out stalls?"

"That's a great idea, now we're cooking." I said, " We can also consolidate everything out in that barn, all the old tractors, harvesters and other implements that aren't essential."

This statement invoked some disapproving looks to which I replied, "Look we are in crisis mode right now, if we don't need it and it doesn't hold any significant sentimental value, we need the money."

A few members were still hesitant, but most gave in and agreed. We began to work out plans to accomplish these new projects. A few family members were placed in charge of finding materials to repair and restore the barn, my cousin volunteered to go to the school to offer the barn up for rent, I volunteered to go get a trailer from the family's company and haul hay to be sold. Things were going great, it seemed that even in this situation we can ban together and still have a good outcome. Then the phone rang.

Leena picked up the land landline and said, "Hello?", "Yes, this is her.", "No, my husband and I are her legal guardians.", "What do you mean she never made it to 2nd period."

I instantly knew the subject of the phone call. My heart sank in my chest like a ton of bricks.

"How do you freaking lose a kid.", "Thank you, I will go look for her."

Leena hung up the phone as I slowly rose from the table and walked towards the back door. I grabbed my cowboy hat and truck keys off the rack, "You all start getting the farm fixed, I'll take care of this situation."

I walked out the back door, and not one person uttered a word as I slammed the door behind me.

<u>Chapter 4</u>

Trying to be a parent to someone who is not your child is difficult. Since undertaking this task, I have developed a new respect for the men who marry single mothers, and women who marry single fathers. In my own personal opinion those couples are the ones I would vote most likely make it to forever, the single accomplishment every couple strives to achieve. Why is that? The outsider coming into the pre-started family not only has the task of creating a romantic relationship with the adult, but also a familial relationship with the children. This requires a lot of love, tact, and patience, the three things most people don't seem to have time for nowadays. The amount of love that flows through that whole chain is astronomical. There truly is no 'one size fits all' solution to parenting. In my case, I have to be Lexi's friend in the sense that we can have fun, and my goal is to make her feel that she can come to me with any problem or even come to me for advice and not feel as if she will be reprimanded. However, I also have to be the parental figure that she lacks in her everyday life by being the barriers guiding her along the right path. Both of these tasks are difficult and require an expert skill I seem to lack, but I manage. It seems tragic to me that

Lexi's real parents couldn't care less about her well-being, it truly blows my mind that you would conceive a child and not know how she's doing from day to day, or even bother to check up on her.

Starting at the high school I drove the side streets and the main road through town to try and locate Lexi. The wind blowing through the truck allowed me to cool my temper. As a kid I too would skip school just to hang out with friends, so I guess, it's not the worst thing in the world, but I also need to make sure she knows that it's not ok.

On my third time down the main strip, I spied her. My heart was relieved until I saw something that made every single dad instinct I had go bananas. Lexi was holding hands with a boy. I realize I said that said skipping wasn't the worst, but I retract that statement. I pulled into a parking spot that was a little way from where they currently were. I just watched them for a moment. Lexi had the biggest smile on her face, she was joking and laughing with this boy, and as I watched him, I saw the complete opposite. She seemed like she was obsessed with him and he could care less, which led me to believe that he had something else planned. They both walked into the grocery store that was a hardware store, and a sandwich shop, oh my. I killed the truck and started that way. The little bell on the door rang as I entered the shop. I noticed that they had gone to the very back and were sitting at the bar, they hadn't seen me walk in. I began to walk through the grocery aisles to the back, just peeking over the top of the shelves to watch. It was breaking my heart to see that she couldn't see through his charade and it infuriated me to see how little he cared for her. I had to stop this.

When I got to the back, Lexi was facing away from my direction. I walked up to the counter and confidently said, "Do y' all know where I can find the headache relief medicine, I've had quite the stressful morning."

Lexi whipped around and every ounce of color drained from her face. We locked eyes for a second before I said, "I'll be out in the truck, you got two minutes." And then I walked away.

A short while later Lexi and the boy came out and walked over the truck. Lexi climbed in looking embarrassed, and the boy came over to the window and knocked. So, I casually rolled it down.

The boy said, "You know she doesn't have to go with you."

Without missing a beat, I opened the center console and pulled out my .45 revolver and set it on the dashboard, "I'm sorry son, I couldn't hear you, you'll have to say that a little louder."

He backed up slowly from the truck as I put it in reverse and backed out on the main road.

I could feel her blue eyes staring into my soul as we drove. But I kept my gaze on the road and didn't say a word. When we got to Starlight Trailer's Warehouse, I backed the truck up to a long flatbed trailer. I climbed out and started hooking it up, Lexi followed but she kept some distance from me. She climbed up on the bed of the truck and secured the gooseneck, attached both chains and the electrical port, just like I taught her. In no time we were on our way back to the farm, not one word uttered between the two of us.

I finally broke the silence, "What the hell is wrong with you?"

"I'm sorry, I just didn't want to go to school today."

"I'm not even mad you skipped school," I said, "everyone needs a mental health day every once in a while, if you would've just said something, I would've hung out with you today."

She just stayed silent, I continued, "I'm mad that you skipped school with a boy who was just using you."

Confused she said, "What are you talking about?"

"I watched y' all for a little bit to see what the heck was going on," I said, "From what I could see, he wasn't there because he likes you like a girlfriend, his fake expressions, the way he avoided holding your hand unless you initiated it, he doesn't care about you, and it was obvious."

She got all offended, "He does like me, you're wrong about him."

"Look I'm not going to fight with you, from a guy's perspective, he was using you."

She turned away and looked out the window as we pulled up the driveway and down to the hay barn. We both climbed out and pulled open the barn doors.

I walked in and examined the hay intently and then I looked over at Lexi, "Look, I know your mad at me right now, but I'm going to stick by what I said until you prove me wrong."

"How am I going to prove you wrong!?" she said angrily.

"Invite him over to have dinner with us, have him take you on a nice date without expecting anything in return, you're a smart girl, I know you can figure it out," I said, "right now though, you are going to help me save this farm."

"What's happening to the farm?" She said.

"We are out of money and we are going to lose this place if we don't do something quick."

"I had no idea, how exactly are we out of money?" She asked, "I overheard Leena and Ryan, saying how great the soybean and corn prices were last year."

"Are you sure?" I asked, "I was under the impression that we got hit hard last year."

"I'm pretty sure, they just kept going on and on about it at their dinner party a couple of weeks ago."

An idea popped in my head, "Lexi, I need you to load as much of this hay onto that trailer as you can, I need to check something out, I'll be back soon."

"Um…ok." She said hesitantly

I rushed out of the barn, unhooked the trailer from the truck, and sped off towards the house. I burst through the back door and went into the office and pulled the files from the last two years. I went to google and researched the prices from the past two years for both soybeans and corn and compared them to the prices on the farm record sheets. My jaw dropped, I reached for my phone and called every family member I could.

"We need to have a meeting right now, get to the farm as quickly as possible."

Chapter 5

Everyone at the table buzzed with uncertainty, I stood at the head with a pile of papers. With everyone present, I was ready to drop a bombshell and blow this whole case wide open. Beads of sweat began to form on my brow as my mind raced.

"Alright, let's begin," I said, "As you all know I've been trying to figure out why we are suddenly out of money, and as a business person I've been absolutely stumped because there was no recognizable reason at first, but it turns out I was looking in the wrong places all along."

Everyone looked bewildered as I paused. I tried to give it a dramatic effect while I shuffled with the papers until I found the record I was looking for.

"Lexi mentioned something about prices for corn and soybeans, which led me to look at the farm records more closely," I help up the records, " On this sheet it says that when we hauled all of the soybeans and corn off this farm we got $8.43 per bushel for soybeans and $3.78 per bushel for corn."

I set the records down and picked up another sheet of paper, "After a simple google search I found that the actual commodity prices at the time our crops reached the market, soybeans were going for $9.91 per bushel and corn was going for $4.28

per bushel, which lead me to do some calculations. Compared to the price on the records and the amount in our bank versus the true outcome of this exchange was a difference of approximately $250,000."

The entire table looked shocked. My cousin Kim spoke up, "So where exactly is all this money?"

I replied, "That is a very good question. I have a theory as to what happened. Since all of us don't look too deeply into the inner mechanisms of this farm's operations there's only one person who takes care of all of these tasks. Rucker."

"Rucker wouldn't be embezzling from this farm; I've known him for years!" Archer said.

"He's the only person who could've gotten away with changing the numbers on these records Archer, nobody at this table has even touched this piece of paper until today. Stop me if I'm wrong, but we all decided to hire a manager so we wouldn't have to do stuff like this. Plus, Archer, if you go back and look, Rucker has been spending money for this farm like we still had all that money."

The debate was getting hot and the tensions in the room were rising.

"You're probably right. But what now?" Archer said.

"Let me contact my attorney back in Texas and figure out what our next move should be. I personally want to sue Rucker and take him for every penny, but without consult from my attorney I feel like that's reckless."

"Call your attorney right now and put him on speaker phone so we can hear what he has to say," Leena said.

I pulled out my phone and dialed my attorney's number. The anticipation was building after each ring. When he finally answered we went into great detail to describe the situation, how we felt, and our thoughts. After a few minutes of processing, he replied with this, "Let me do some digging, and I'll get back to you, but for now, you need to release him from his employment at the farm without giving any hints that you know about what he's done. Does that make sense?"

"Yes! I read you loud and clear, we will do that today." I said.

"Great! The sooner the better, I'll see you when you get back to Texas."

▪▪▪▪▪▪▪▪▪▪▪▪▪▪▪▪▪▪▪▪▪▪▪▪▪▪▪▪▪▪▪▪▪▪▪▪▪

Hay dust filled my senses, Lexi and I had finished loading the trailer by the time sun was starting to set low on the ridge. A set of headlights came down from the house to the hay barn. It was Archer and Rucker.

Rucker came over and firmly shook my hand and I reciprocated and smiled, "That's quite the load you're hauling there,"

"Yes sir! I figured I would get a few things done around here while I'm up for the weekend, clear out some space for more hay this year."

"Smart man! Archer tells me that you've made quite the name for yourself back in Texas."

"My intelligence is a gift and a curse, the people I do business with would have to agree with that."

He chuckled, "Well congratulations, I know your family here is very proud of you."

"Thank you, that means a lot. Look, the reason we called you down here is to just talk about some things the whole family has been talking about."

"Of course, what's on your mind?"

"Well, I've been looking for a new challenge, and my girlfriend and I have thought about moving up here full-time," I said, "Which means I'll be taking over operations here at the farm. You've done a great job here and I know my Uncle would thank you for keeping his dream alive, but we no longer will need a farm manager."

"Oh, I'm sorry to hear that, I love this job, but I understand," Rucker said, "Family farms should be run by the family, that's always been my policy, but thank you for letting me work for yours"

"Of course! And you're always welcome here." I smiled the fakest smile I could muster up.

Archer and Rucker drove back up to the house, and Lexi and I got in the truck loaded down with hay. As I got the truck started and the headlights on, I asked Lexi, "What time do you get out of school tomorrow?"

"Tomorrow is teacher in-service, so school is canceled."

I looked at her doubtfully.

"What?" she said, "I'll show you on the school's website."

"Let me get this straight. You skipped school today when you have a free day tomorrow?" I said.

"Yes, what's the problem?"

I just shook my head and pulled away from the hay barn, "Tomorrow you're going with me to Sioux Falls to drop this off."

"Yes sir!" she laughed.

That 4 o'clock alarm came earlier than expected. I groaned as the warm sheet begged me to stay and finally I clambered out of bed. The hardwood floor was cold to the touch on the way to the bathroom. I let the warm water rain down on me and pound my face. When I got dressed I shuffled down the stairs into the living room where Lexi was sleeping, I had to laugh a little when I turned the lamp on, Lexi was hanging halfway off the couch.

I not so subtly tried to wake her up by shaking her, "Wake-up! We have a big day ahead of us, I hope you're not planning on sleeping the day away!"

She rolled over, clicked the home button on her phone and groaned, "Dude, its 4:30 in the morning."

"I know! We should already be on the road!"

"You're nuts," She said sitting up and rubbing her eyes groggily, "I want my bed back, this couch sucks."

"That's what happens when you have a bunch of family members gathered in a location with no hotel," I said as I stepped into the kitchen, "Don't wake Robyn when you go get ready."

After a nice steaming cup of coffee and a donut, I was ready to go. I walked out to the truck and looked out over the field to see the violet colors of the sky starting to make themselves known just beyond the tops of the corn. Lexi came out and go into the truck looking like a zombie.

I offered her some of my coffee, "Here, drink some of that, it'll help get your morning started."

She looked disgusted at the thought, "Um, no, coffee is for old people."

"How rude, I am not old."

She laughed. I put the truck in gear and pulled out of the drive, I could feel every shake or rumble the trailer made behind me as we sped up. Within fifteen minutes of being on the road, Lexi was already slumped over against the window asleep.

What she said though, did give me some things to think about. I understand I'm still young, but I'm not getting any younger. Kaitlyn is my whole world; this is the girl I want to spend the rest of my life with. When we first met in college to now, she truly was the perfect half that made me whole. From a young age, Kaitlyn was always told that she wouldn't be able to successfully carry a child, and when we got together, she was so afraid I wouldn't want her when I found out. Honestly, that had no bearing on my love for her.

The sun had risen enough to fill the pastures with golden rays of light. My eyes glanced over at a farm where I saw a family out doing chores and having fun while doing it, how I longed for something like that. I looked over at Lexi and how smushed her face looked against the window. Then it hit me. A little idea.

<u>Chapter 6</u>

The rest of my trip to Nebraska was uneventful and packed full of work. For now, the farm was surviving and on track to recovery. The drive back to my home was one that I have done a thousand times. However, each time I made the trip there was always new buildings or restaurants to see. I was hyper-aware of the increasing encroachment of the city towards my little town. Every day a new house pops up or a new neighborhood development goes into production. Kaitlyn and I are lucky though, we live on the side of the lake that backs up to a nature preserve, so we will never experience construction for the duration of our time here.

I turned into our long snaking driveway, crossed through the front gate and over the cattle guard. All the trees lining the driveway prevented anyone from seeing the house or the barns. I loved the privacy it gave us. As we were quickly approaching summer, all the trees were canopied over the truck. The driveway opened up into a large open area where you could go right to the barn or left to the house. I turned my wheels hard to the left and stopped just short of the front porch. I then gathered my things and walked through the front door.

"Hey baby, I'm home," I yelled into the house.

Kaitlyn poked her head out of the kitchen. She excitedly gasped and ran towards the front door. Before I had any idea of what happened, she had jumped into my arms and wrapped her legs around me. Her arms were vice-like around my neck and her blonde hair filled my senses with the smell of coconuts. When she finally loosened, she leaned her head back and looked into my eyes. Kaitlyn smiled and leaned in to kiss my lips gently. She ran her fingers through my hair and across my cheeks. Climbing down, Kaitlyn looked into my eyes one more time before biting her lip. She started to blush as she grabbed my hand and led me upstairs.

Since I've been home Kaitlyn has not left my side. Today, we decided to go out to a quick lunch before I met with my attorney, so I could really lay out the scope of what happened and to propose my little idea to her. To be completely honest I was extremely nervous. Would she think I was crazy? Would she think I was pushing too far? Or would she be completely on board?

The band Flatland Cavalry provided the background music for our truck ride into town. I could feel Kaitlyn staring into my soul, and every time I looked over at her, she quickly turned her head and pretended to be looking out the window. Finally, I asked, "What?"

"Oh, nothing." She replied with a smile.

For the time being, I dropped it. But she just kept staring, so more intently I asked, "What?"

"Nothing!" She said as she bit her lip. I just smiled and rolled my eyes.

"How are you so attractive?" She asked, "Like how is it that God can create such an attractive human-being, how can some like you even exist?"

I laughed, "I have no idea who you're talking about, but it's sure as heck, not me."

She then reached over and punched my arm with all the strength she could muster, "How dare you say that about yourself, you're the most handsome being to ever walk this earth you know."

"I love you, but that was so cheesy." I laughed again.

"Laugh at this." She then unbuckled her seatbelt and climbed on the center console to get closer to me. She then began to kiss my cheek and work her way down to my neck, then collarbone.

"You're going to get us in a wreck."

She replied definitively with, "Oh well."

We successfully made it to the restaurant with minimal swerving. Kaitlyn's favorite place to eat is a small marina restaurant on the lake that has patio seating looking out over the water. It was small and few people knew about it, to us it was the best-kept secret in town. I had been pondering how I would deliver my idea to her, but I couldn't decide how. I looked out across the water to see if the waves could provide some guidance.

Once we got our food, Kaitlyn picked out the perfect place to eat. I sat down and just looked her over. Her long blond hair with subtle curls was pulled back into a ponytail. This exposed her pale flush skin and the stripe of freckles that you could barely see ran from cheekbone to cheekbone. Her eyes were the color of the purest ocean, it melted my heart every time I looked upon them. In our relationship, we have had a handful of fights, and I have not won a single one, it's hard to stay mad at someone who throws the weight of the world behind two beautiful eyes, and deep down I know she uses that to her advantage.

"Hey, Kaitlyn?" I said.

She unfolded her napkin and laid it delicately on her lap, "Yes?"

"What if," it was hard to muster up the words, "we adopted a kid?"

She just stared at me. I began to worry.

"Don't play games like that." She said brushing it off.

I reached across the table and grabbed her hands, "Kaitlyn, I'm serious."

Tears started to well up in her eyes as she jumped across the table, knocking over drinks and hugged me to the point where I couldn't breathe.

"Is that a yes?" I managed to get out.

"Yes! Yes, a million times!" she sobbed into my shirt.

She looked up at me with puffy eyes, "I think I have someone in mind, she could use a good stable home."

"That's actually what I was going ask you, I also have someone in mind too," I said.

"Is it Lexi?" She asked.

"Yes, how did you know?!"

"Because that's exactly who I was thinking of."

We both kissed and hugged each other hard. She finally released me and sat back in her seat. My heart was so happy, and I know hers was too. Best lunch ever.

■■■■■■■■■■■■■■■■■■■■■■■■■■■■■■■■■■

My attorney got up at the front of the conference room to give me a presentation of his findings. Personally, I enjoyed presentations, it put all the information I needed to know in a need and fun format. I know, I'm weird.

"Alright," he started, "I've done some digging, and while the option to sue him is still on the table, I have some information for you that might make you reconsider."

He clicked the slide, "While I'm sure you are aware that Starlight Trailer's major competitor Brumfield

Aluminum, who is also is based out of the same town, has been killing Starlight Trailers in sales for the past few decades until a few years ago. After some digging, I found that your farm manager owns a significant chunk of Brumfield Trailers."

"This is making zero sense," I said.

"I'm getting there," my attorney said, " The reason he owns a significant portion, about 30%, is because his family owns the trailer company."

"What does any of this have to do with the farm?"

"If you would stop interrupting me, you'd find out."

"That's fair."

"They were killing your family in sales is because they were importing cheap aluminum from foreign countries while Starlight Trailers kept an American based contract. When President Trump got elected to office two years ago, he slapped on the tariffs for non-American made imports. This effectively hurt Brumfield trailers because they couldn't find a cheap aluminum contract."

He clicked the slide to a downward trending graph, "This is Brumfield's sales in the past two years, they are barely hanging on by a thread. I can positively say that the money embezzled from the farm was going to Brumfield to keep it afloat."

On the next slide had a chart showed a couple of documents.

I interrupted, "His credit is absolutely wrecked! He has two mortgages out on his house?"

"Yes sir so does his parents," he said, "There is no major bank that will go near them."

I nodded while the gears in my head turned, "They have leveraged every penny into this company. When I let him go from the farm that really screwed him over."

He clicked over to the next slide to reveal charts from the stock market. My jaw dropped, "Holy shit, I'm not this lucky."

My attorney smiled, "I just saw that little lightbulb turn on."

"Look at this," I said, "Two years ago they were sitting at $156.35 a share and today it's sitting at $3.27 per share."

We looked at each other intently, "I'm going to ruin his life with a smile on my face."

"Welcome back," he said, "It's been a while since I've seen this side of you."

"When you push on me, I'm going to push back harder, and he's about to learn that lesson the hard way. This man is going to learn the hard way not to mess with me and my family."

<u>Chapter 7</u>

"So, what are you going to do?" Kaitlyn asked.

I veered my horse back onto the trail as Kaitlyn and I rode side-by-side, "Well, I have a plan going right now, but I will end up needed a little help, I don't have enough money at the moment."

"Just ask Daddy, I'm sure he'll help you," she said, "You know he thinks you can do no wrong."

"As much as I hate asking your father for things, I may just end up doing that."

We came across the top of the hill that overlooked my small property. You could see for miles on either side, it was truly breathtaking.

"You know," Kaitlyn started, "the first time I saw you doing this kind of business stuff, it scared me."

I looked over at her confused, "Why were you scared?"

"I'm not completely sure," she took a second to mull it over, "the way you fight people, not with violence but instead, through the power of your brain scared me."

I tilted my head still utterly confused, she continued, "The way you know the law and use it to your advantage, the way you study a person and pick apart everything about them, and the way you do all of it so flawlessly and effortlessly scared me because I didn't understand it all."

"Baby, I never try to intentionally destroy someone unless they deserve it."

"And I understand that now, but in the beginning, it was scary," She laughed, "once you told me about your childhood and how hard it was for you going up, everything began to make sense."

"Being this way takes a toll and I'm getting tired." I said, "it's not a great life to live when you constantly are at war with someone or something."

"Can you make me a promise?" she asked.

"Sure," I replied.

"After your finished, will you retire from this lifestyle? Will you

think about settling down and having
a normal life?"

She looked at me with those beautiful
eyes. I knew I had been beaten,
"Kaitlyn Elise, I promise that when
I'm finished with the last venture, I
will settle down and have a normal
life."

"Good, I'm going to hold you
to it." She smiled.
■■■■■■■■■■■■■■■■■■■■■■■■■■■■■■■■■■■■

I straightened my suit vest and
adjusted my cowboy hat. I casually
looked over the menu waiting for
Kaitlyn's father to arrive. I had
scheduled a dinner with him to
discuss the plan I had. Kaitlyn's
father, Mark, was a very large man.
And when I say large, I mean both
vertically and horizontally. Normally,
I'm never intimidated by anyone, that
was until I met Mark. He was an
executive at Exxon-Mobil, the money
that family possesses is of an

unlimited supply it seems. Kaitlyn's family owns a mansion worth almost six million dollars and a massive cattle ranch just north of Dallas worth almost eleven million dollars. When I first got to know Kaitlyn, she led me on to believe her family was dirt poor, which is why when she first took me home to meet her parents, I was shocked to find out the complete opposite.

I spied Mark walk in and over to the table. I stood up to greet and shake his monstrous hand.

"How are you doing sir," I said, "it's always a pleasure to see you!"

"The pleasure is all mine young man," Mark replied as we sat down.

We both ordered Whisky and some food and had some nice conversations about his work and how Kaitlyn's mom and sister were doing.

"Alright son," Mark said, "Tell me everything about this situation you're in."

I went into great detail to explain to him exactly what had happened over the course of the past week. I then proceeded to tell him about the information I found out through my attorney. He seemed very interested in how I was going to resolve the problem, so I extensively laid out every single detailed I had planned for my endgame. Nothing seemed to phase Mark in the few years that I've known him but when I got finished laying my big plan, he smiled.

"That's why I came here today to ask for some help." I finished.

"You know, I've always like you, and this plan you have is exactly why I'm more than happy to help you."

"Thank you, sir." I smiled.

"Of course," he said, "Tomorrow I'll get all this moving for you."

"Just let me know what you hear, Kaitlyn and I are flying up to Nebraska tomorrow to catch Lexi's band concert and do some work around the farm."

"I'll drink to that." He said finishing that last of the whiskey in his glass.

"Also, sir, I have one more thing I need to talk to you about."

▪▪▪▪▪▪▪▪▪▪▪▪▪▪▪▪▪▪▪▪▪▪▪▪▪▪▪▪▪▪▪▪▪▪▪

Another thing I despise in this world is airport security. Every time I go to the airport it seems this circus is more and more irritating. They make you take off your shoes, but somehow always get pissed off at me when I get horse poop or dirt inside the tubs. They make you take off your belt, so now, not only are my pants halfway hanging off my butt, but the smart-ass security people always have to make a comment on my belt buckle. I've heard everything from 'Do you get satellite reception on that thing?' to 'Is something of that size really necessary?.'' I understand the need for security, but I just wished it wasn't such a hassle.

Because I'm a gentleman I always offer to carry Kaitlyn's bags. This is a mistake every time. When I travel, I try and pack as lightly as possible, especially when I go to the farm because I already have a handful of outfits up there already. Kaitlyn, on the other hand, has four bags, at least one is for shoes, another is for shirts and pants, another is for undies, bras, and belts, and finally, she has one bag dedicated to make-up, toiletries, and jewelry. The jewelry bag and shoe bag are always the heaviest. But I love her and do it without complaining. Correction, I do it without complaining out loud.

I plopped down in the seat close to the terminal while we waited for our flight. I could feel my phone vibrating in my pocket, so I quickly wiggled an arm out from under a bag and answered, "Hello?"

"You'll never guess what just happened." I recognized Mark's voice on the other end of the line.

"What happened?!" I said I was a little concerned at his tone.

"I submitted two offers to both parties and within two hours they both accepted," he said, "they must be desperate because I went even lower than the price we had discussed."

"Wow, that's shocking. At least things are starting off in the right direction."

"They are sending over the paperwork shortly; they are trying to expedite this process as quickly as possible."

"This is just too easy Mark," I said, Kaitlyn, whipped her head around and mouthed the words 'is that my dad?' and I nodded.

"Keep doing what you're doing son, I'm here for you if you want more help."

"Thank you, sir." I barely got the words out before Kaitlyn ripped the phone out of my hands.

"Hi daddy!" she said into the phone.

I couldn't hear what was happening on the other end but after a few minutes Kaitlyn was finished, and she hung up. My plan was right on track.

When it was our turn, I walked over and checked in all the bags. I then turned to Kaitlyn and interlaced my fingers in hers as we walked down the corridor and onto the plane.

<u>Chapter 8</u>

Walking out of the tiny airport in Omaha the bright sun obstructed my view at first. This is why when someone ran up and almost tackled me, I was caught so off guard. When I regained my balance, it was to my surprise to see Lexi attached to my waist.

"Hey, sweet girl," I said smiling.

"I know it's only been two weeks, but it's felt like forever." She said.

I laughed as she detached from me and went and hugged Kaitlyn just as hard.

A thought hit me out of nowhere, "How did you get here?"

Lexi replied, "Leena drove the truck up here to pick you two up."

"How thoughtful, why didn't you drive?" I said.

"She wouldn't let me drive, but can I drive home?!" she said, "I promise I've been driving the truck around the farm for practice."

I looked at Kaitlyn who was smiling from ear to ear and said to Lexi, "Well if you're going to drive us home, we have to get to the truck first."

Lexi jumped up and said, "Yes!" with a fist pump in the air.

Overall letting Lexi drive wasn't a bad idea, it just wasn't the best idea I've ever had. I was white knuckle gripping the armrest the first hour of the drive. Finally, I told her to pull over so we could 'get gas' but really, I was just wanted to switch drivers. She seemed happy to drive at all.

"What time do you need to be at the school for warm up?" I asked her.

"I need to be there at 6," she said.

I looked at the clock on the dash, "Girl it's already almost 5, we're going to be cutting it close."

"Oh well, at least I got to come to get you two."

I rolled my eyes and eased on the accelerator a little harder.

The concert was spectacular. Lexi was dressed in an awful felt dress, just like the ones the girls had to wear when I was in high school, but I kept that opinion to myself. I felt like such a dad, taking pictures and waving to her. Watching her play each of the pieces with such enthusiasm made my heart swell with pride. I reached over and rested my hand on Kaitlyn's inner thigh as she wrapped her arm around mine and rested her head against my shoulder.

After the concert, Kaitlyn and I took Lexi to get some ice cream. When we got our dessert and sat down, Kaitlyn and I sat on one side of the booth and Lexi sat on the other. We talked about her schooling and what she wanted to be someday. We laughed and had a good time. I knew Kaitlyn was ready to pop the question to Lexi when she reached under the table and grabbed my hand.

"Hey Lex, Kaitlyn and I were talking, and we have something to talk to you about."

"Okay? What is it?" Lexi replied.

"Well, do you like it here in Nebraska ?" I asked.

"I mean it's not the worst place to live."

"How would you feel about living somewhere else? More specifically Texas?" Kaitlyn said.

"Like living with you guys?"

"Yes, that's where we were going with all that," I said, "Lexi, what if Kaitlyn and I adopted you and had you move to Texas with us?"

Stunned Lexi said, "Aw man, I don't know."

Kaitlyn quickly replied, "You don't have to give an answer right now, it was just a thought.

"Okay!" she smiled and continued eating her ice cream.

Later that night, Kaitlyn and I were lying in bed and I thought I heard a soft whimper. I rolled over the see if she was still awake and in the soft light of the moon coming through the window I could see her tear stained face.

I mustered up some groggy words, "Baby, what's wrong?"

"What if she doesn't choose us?" Kaitlyn said quivering her lip.

"If she doesn't choose us, there are plenty of other children out there for us to adopt, when I suggested this to you, I wasn't saying this one kid is our only option. Kaitlyn, I want to have a family with you someday, I want to build a life with you."

She started crying harder but this time out of happiness, she wrapped her arms around me and whispered in my ear, "I love you." And I whispered back, "I love you more."

. . . .

The best thing about being at the farm was the luxury of quality home cooked meals. Without the various fast food restaurants available here, it forces families to sit and interact. In my personal opinion, you can learn more about someone by the way they eat. How do they conduct themselves at the table? Do they have quality manners? Do they scarf down every last bite as quickly as they can? Or are they more prone to taking long thoughtful chews and enjoying each and every bite? For the fast eater, these people are inclined to live a fast-paced, almost reckless, life; they most likely don't think through their decisions and act hastily. For the slow eaters, these individuals like to take the slow lane in life; they most likely take longer than they should when making decisions. These observations are just some that I've made over the years. In most social groups my acute observations have been labeled 'weird' so I mostly keep them to myself.

Between bites of overly syrupy pancake, Archer implored me, "What makes you think you can win against him?"

"Simply put, I don't lose," I said.

Everyone at the table laughed except Kaitlyn. She knew that what I was saying was right.

"Let me put it like this," Archer said, "How are you going to get our money back?"

"You'll see," I said, "If we would've filed a lawsuit, we wouldn't have seen a single penny. The entire family is so far broke just trying to keep that company afloat."

"I hope you're right."

"Trust me, nobody hurts my family and walks away unscathed," I said standing up, "When I'm done with them, they'll be lucky to have two nickels to rub together. I'm chopping their family tree down." I took Kaitlyn's plate and my own to the sink and began washing them. Everyone at the table was still stunned.

"You need to have mercy on them, there's no need to be cruel," Archer said.

I slowly looked up and turned off the sink before locking eyes with Archer, "I believe in choices. When they stole from us, that was a choice.

But you're right, I'll be merciful. I'll give them one last choice. I hope they make the right one."

Chapter 9

Planting a quick kiss on Kaitlyn's forehead, I pulled the covers closer to her body. When I reached the back door, I was careful not to wake Lexi who was fast asleep on the couch. I slowly twisted the knob and gently pulled back the creaky old door so I could slip out unseen. When I made it the truck I sighed deeply and turned the ignition.

On a Saturday night, the only thing to do in town was to go to the only bar within 50 miles. And that's exactly where I went. When I walked in, the smoke-filled atmosphere almost corrupted the neon glow that befell the place. I took a seat at the bar and ordered my usual poison of choice. The way it burned my throat took the edge off of any situation. As much as I wanted to just keep drinking I had to stay razor sharp, I was here on a mission hoping my prey would come out to the watering hole to drink.

A young lady, close to my age, came up to me and said, "Hey cowboy, are you new around here?"

I spied my target enter in through the door and take a seat at the opposite end of the bar from me. But I decided to watch him from afar.

"I'm not from around here."

"That's probably why I don't recognize you." She laughed.

"Probably not, I'm from Texas," I replied.

"Well, you look really good in neon." She said moving in closer.

"Who doesn't," I replied with a smile. I got up and made my way to the other end of the bar where I took a seat next to him.

"Hey, Rucker," I said after ordering another drink.

"Hey!," he said, "How are you doing sir?"

I smiled, "Just looking to get out of the house, relax a little."

"I understand that I've been running myself into the dirt lately, you want a smoke?"

I grabbed one out of the pack and lit it up. Taking a long drag, it reminded me of my high school rodeo days. I blew the smoke out slowly.

Rucker did the same. We sat in silence for a little while.

I broke the silence, "Congratulations on selling your house."

He looked at me in udder confusion, "How did you know that?"

"News gets around in a small town I guess." I smiled.

"It just happened yesterday, there's no way you could've known."

"Rucker, let's not play games anymore."

"What games? What are you talking about?"

I took another drag and blew, "You hurt my family Rucker, and now it's my turn to hurt you."

His face turned beet red, "How did you find out?"

"It wasn't that hard buddy."

"So, what are you going to do? Sue me?"

"Nah, that's way too easy." I said, "Having my father-in-law buy your house and your parents' house for nickels and dimes of the true value isn't my idea of hurting you." He continued to just sit in silence.

"My father-in-law is going to plow over both properties and erect a beautiful gas station," I said taking another drag, "It's genius really, there's not a gas station within 25 miles of both properties."

The more I kept talking the madder he got, "My idea of hurting you is going to be Monday morning when the stock market opens, and I purchase every single share of Brumfield Trailers you and your parents have for sale. Your family will have the unique distinction of being the first generation to lose the company that your great grandparents fought so hard to start. You're going to lose the company at the hands of a twenty-one-year-old kid. I'm only telling you this cause I know there's nothing you can do to stop it."

He got up and began to put on his jacket and I continued, "I suggest finding someone to give you the money to keep the company afloat and prevent me from taking over because you won't like what the company looks like when I'm at the helm. And honestly Rucker, I hope you do find someone who's dumb enough to give you the money because this has just been too fucking easy."

As he turned to walk away, he whipped around, "You will regret ever having met me."

"No, Rucker," I said, "Regret is the one thing I just won't do."
∎∎∎∎∎∎∎∎∎∎∎∎∎∎∎∎∎∎∎∎∎∎∎∎∎∎∎∎∎∎∎∎∎∎∎∎∎

I opened my eyes to find myself in an unfamiliar landscape. I was standing in the middle of a field. The full moon illuminated the grain that was at least mid-thigh level in height. I looked around and noticed a cluster of trees to my left, and to my right was what looked like mountains, but closer to the hill country in Texas. In the distance, I spied a large white house and white barns lit up. I started walking towards the direction of the house to try and figure out where I was.

Suddenly on my right, the wheat field erupted into a plume of flames. The heat was intense and every instinct inside me screamed to run. But I was frozen. The left side of the field erupted into flames. Why couldn't I run? I did a quick turn and flames surrounded me.

There was a quick break in the fire, and it split down the middle to reveal a team of men using flamethrowers to torch the field. What was going on! My heart pounded faster and faster until it felt like it was going to explode from my chest. I blinked slowly and when I opened my eyes I was in a luxury office standing in front of a neat modern desk, all the papers were neatly stacked, and the computer was expensive looking. Seated at the desk was a woman with strawberry blond hair, who stared at me with a stern face expecting an answer.

"I'm sorry?" I said. There was a persistent ringing in my ears.

"I said, loyalty, morality, reason, these things don't apply to you do they?" She asked.

My brain wanted to say, "No those things have always applied to me."

But the words that came out were, "Not anymore."

The lady at the desk gave me a devilish grin, "I knew I liked you, unlike most you have the balls to do what needs to be done."

I slowly blinked again. The ringing ceased and when I reopened eyes I was standing in front of the white house and the white barns. The front door opened and a girl with sandy blonde hair looked me up and down with wide eyes.

"Daddy, what happened to you!" She proclaimed.

I had no control over my actions, it felt as if I was watching a movie. I started walking up the front steps into the house and I uttered,

"It's a product of war my dear." I continued on to a gorgeous kitchen. When I arrived at a sink I reached underneath and pulled out a first-aid kit. I pulled out some sutures and went to a bathroom.

When I looked in the mirror I didn't recognize who the man in the mirror was at first. It was me. The weathered skin coupled with little grey hairs coming in was a horrific image. Along my hairline, there was a long cut that was trickling blood onto my face. I blinked again.

This time when I opened my eyes I was inside an elevator. The metal on the door reflected my image. I was back to the same thin twenty-one-year-old kid, I was in a suit and cowboy hat. The elevator played the somber tune of Uncle Lucius entitled *Keep the Wolves Away*. The longer I stood on the elevator the more and more it became clear that the ride was never-ending. I wanted to try and press the emergency button or try a floor button, but my body was stiff as a rod.

Finally, I felt the elevator slowing down. When the elevator stopped the doors didn't open at first. I just sat there in a non-moving elevator. Suddenly, I heard the ding that let me know I had arrived on my floor of choice. The doors slowly opened to reveal a man standing in front of the entrance. I tried to move to get out of the elevator, but my body was still stiff. I watched the man stare at me. His facial features seemed fuzzy. Like watching a show that has nudity blurred out in it. After a while, he raised his right hand and put it across his body into his jacket. My heart sank to my stomach. I tried to squirm and move but every attempt was futile. The man pulled out a gun. A short, sleek, black gun and pointed it at me. When he fired I felt a sharp pain in my chest. My ears rang and liquid filled my hands as I clutched my chest.

■■■■■■■■■■■■■■■■■■■■■■■■■■■■■■■■■■■■■

A loud gunshot and a sharp pain in my chest caused me to spring up in bed. When I recovered my breath, I looked around to find that it was all just a lucid dream. Sweat was pouring from my brow. I was so worked up I hardly noticed Kaitlyn was awake too trying to figure out what was wrong with me.

"Baby, what's the matter?" she kept asking.

I finally came to my senses and replied, "It's nothing, just a nightmare."

"What was it about?" She asked.

"I'm not quite sure, it was very confusing."

"Why do you smell like smoke?"

"I went to the bar to confront Rucker Davis."

"Please tell me you didn't."

"I gave him a choice, surrender or face complete and udder destruction."

"I love you, and I'll stand by you no matter what, but that was not a smart thing to do."

"I love you too, but it was better than just taking over his family's company without them knowing what was coming."

"Sometimes I just don't understand why you do the things you do."

I laid back down and rolled over to face the wall, "Nobody ever does."

She put her tiny arms around as much my body as she could and kissed the back of my head, "That doesn't mean I don't want to learn though."

I smiled.

Chapter 10

Monday morning, I was up at 6:45 just like every other morning but at least I was in my own bed. The flight back to Texas was just like every other one, it gave me time to think. My laptop was set up on the front porch and it was already monitoring the stock market. At 8 am we would see whether or not he took my advice. I walked out to the barn and fed the horses, the dusty barn welcomed me with warm morning sunlight beaming in. The sound of birds chirped and horses snorting filled the morning air.

As I finished feeding a new sound caught my attention. The sound of a car. I heard the sound of tires crossing the cattle guard at the front entrance. Since the house and barn were tucked behind a curtain of trees, I couldn't see the road coming in. I could still hear the sound of a car creeping up the gravel road. I ran back to the house and burst through the front door. I grabbed my Winchester .30.30 Lever Action Rifle and made my way back to the porch. I was shocked to see that it was a yellow taxi. As the car emerged from the trees and stopped just short of the house I watched intensely as someone fumbled around in the back seat. The door opened and a pair of small boots hit the ground and a girl with sleek brown hair climbed out.

It was Lexi. But something was different. Under her right eye, there was a giant bruise. When she gathered her things and put them on the ground as the taxi pulled away, she ran to the porch and hugged me as hard as she could with tears running down her face.

"Sweet girl," I said hugging her back, "What are you doing here?!"

Through muffled sobs, she said, "My father got drunk…sniff… he came to the farm last night and hit me…sniff… nobody was home, and he broke stuff… sniff…he was mad that mother left."

My heart just broke for this girl, "Where is he now? Why did your mom leave?"

"The police came…sniff… they took him to jail…sniff…he said mom left because she doesn't love me or him…sniff…he said I was the worst thing that ever happened to them."

"Oh no," I rubbed her back, then I got down on one knee so that way I could be at eye-level with her, "Look at me, you are the best thing to happen to anyone, do you understand me? Kaitlyn and I love you so much, the rest of the family loves you too."

She just hugged my neck. I could feel her tears soaking my shoulder, "Alright, let's get your stuff."

We went and grabbed her bag and took them inside the house. Putting all her bags in the living room, I went to wake Kaitlyn up. I shook her awake and she was not happy.

"Kaitlyn. Kaitlyn. Wake up."

"What the hell do you want?" she said groggily.

"Put on some clothes we have a visitor, hurry."

"What? Who?" she asked as she climbed out of bed, "What should I wear?"

"Just put these on," I said throwing her a pair of my sweatpants.

We rushed downstairs like it was Christmas morning. When we reached the bottom, I saw that Lexi had curled up with a blanket on the couch and she was fast asleep. At first, Kaitlyn didn't see her but when she finally saw all the bags and Lexi passed out on the couch, she covered her mouth with her hand and one single tear ran down from her cheek.

• •

"That's when I said to him, 'I suggest finding someone to give you the money to keep the company afloat and prevent me from taking over because you won't like what the company looks like when I'm at the helm. And honestly Rucker, I hope you do find someone who's dumb enough to give you the money because this has just been too fucking easy' and by looking at this he tried his hardest because stocks went from $3.00 to $5.50 per share since the stock market opened this morning."

"So, what are you going to do?" Kaitlyn said.

"Well' I'll keep monitoring it, but chances are he got enough cash to raise it this high and in a few hours it'll go back down."

"What's going to happen when you own over half this company?"

"It's all a part of the plan," I said giving her a devilish smile.

The front screen door opened, and Lexi came out rubbing her eyes.

"Well hello sleepy head," I said, "We thought you were going to sleep the whole day away."

She smiled and walked over to hug Kaitlyn, "It was kind of hard to sleep in an airport."

"Pull up a rocker, we have a few questions for you."

She went and brought a rocker from the opposite side of the porch. I could see the deep purple and green in her bruise, and it infuriated me to think about what she went through last night. When she sat down in the rocker I asked, "How did you get here?"

"Well, first I drove your truck to the airport."

I cut her off, "Timeout. You illegally drove my truck to the airport?"

"Yes, sir." She said all embarrassed, "But don't worry your truck is fine."

"I don't even know what to say to that because I have so many things to say, continue with your story."

"When I got to the airport I was able to buy a ticket for the last flight to DFW Airport."

I interrupted again, "Pause. How did you get the money to buy a plane ticket and how did you know to come to Fort Worth?

"When my father came over he dropped his wallet on the ground, and inside he had $500 cash, so I used the money to buy a plane ticket and food at T.G.I. Fridays at the airport. I also took a picture of your address in Leena's address book and plugged it into the map's app on my phone. When I got to DFW Airport I called Leena to tell them I was alright."

"So, let me get this straight. You stole money, ran away from home and illegally drove a truck that's not yours to the airport where you bought a plane ticket to come to Texas? Honey, you're like 0-4 right now in terms of morality."

"I know, I'm really sorry but I couldn't think of any other option."

" I get it, but you could've called us."

"I didn't want to wake you guys up last night, that's why when I got here at 2 am I just tried to sleep in the airport until 6 am."

I smacked my forehead, "You spent the night at the airport?! We would've come and gotten you silly, or at least I would have, sleeping beauty over here would've been snoring."

Lexi laughed, and Kaitlyn was not amused, "Hey! How rude, if anything I would've been woken up by all the racket you make when moving around the house."

She laughed harder, and it made me smile to see her happy. She pointed at my laptop and asked, "What are you doing?"

"I am about to perform a hostile takeover of a company whose owners stole money from our family."

"Cool," She said holding out the 'o' sound, "How are you doing that?"

So I explained, "Well this here is the stock market, the chart right here," I pointed at the graph in the middle of the screen, "Shows how the company is doing over a span of time, the line on the graph represents how much the company is worth 'per share."

"What is a share?"

"When a company gets big enough or cool enough, the company is divided into pieces for people who pay money to own a share of that company."

"So, is this company doing good?"

I pointed at the highest part of the graph, "Right here is where the company did the best over its lifetime and that was two years ago, the company was worth about $160 per share." I traced my finger down the steep slope all the way to the end, "This right here is where the company is at right now its worth $5.50 per share."

"I'd rather have the bigger amount of money." She said.

I chuckled, "I think we all would; the reason that the owners of this company were stealing from our family is that they were not doing so well. They thought by stealing it was the best way to help themselves, kind of like how you stole from your father thinking it was the best way to help yourself."

Her face turned red with embarrassment, I continued, "There's always a better solution, and I'm punishing them for stealing from us by taking over their company."

"Are you going to punish me?" she asked.

"Not this time sweet girl, but let this be a lesson to you that actions have consequences. And consequences aren't always bad, but make sure you evaluate every decision you make from here on out."

"Yes, sir." She said looking down at her boots.

"You know, I was thinking," I said, "I really want to go horseback riding today, how does that sound to you?"

Lexi instantly picked her head up, "Can we really!"

Kaitlyn chimed in, "How about some breakfast first?"

Lexi grabbed her stomach and said, "That sounds really good."

"How about I show you to your new room and you can unpack while I make some breakfast."

Lexi nodded and went into the house. Kaitlyn slowly rose from her rocker. She came over and kissed my head, "You're going to be such a good father figure. I think I'm starting to finally understand you."

"We'll see about that," I said.

Before I went inside the house I picked up my laptop. Like I had predicted the stock prices plummeted, and sooner than I thought. Right, that instant I purchased of 30,000 shares of Brumfield Trailers. I was now the proud owner of 60% of a disaster. I smiled, closed my laptop, and walked inside to my new family.

I know what you might be thinking. 'This is definitely the end of the story' and I can assure you that we still have a little way to go before the completion of this book. After all, you have to see how I finish up my plan.

Chapter 11

It's been two months since my takeover of Brumfield Trailers. Today was my first board of directors meeting and I was excited. I have spent the past week crafting a piece of artwork. The paper I had typed was over twelve pages detailing what my plans for the company were. Yesterday I flew up to the farm to have an extra day to get ready. Since the meeting was at Brumfield Trailers headquarters based out of St. Cloud I figured I could meet with a few other board members and tour the production plant. Regrettably, I was the only one to show up for the tour. Thankfully when I arrived at the meeting in St. Cloud everyone was present.

The elevator ride up to the conference room was a lonely one, but when the door opened I was flooded with people who wanted to shake my hand and take my picture. Before I even reached the meeting room I met a handful of other board members who thought it was on their best interest to get acquainted with the new majority stockholder. It never hurt to be a suck-up if it meant that some of your ideas might be considered. But none of that mattered, I was here for one reason and that was to run this company.

When I entered the large meeting room the blank white walls and bright lighting made the room distasteful. Walking down the center aisle there were about ten rows of seats with ten chairs in each row. I then made my way up the front to a raised half moon shaped panel. It was like being a courtroom with many judges. I spied my place at the center. Being a majority stockholder has its perks, they even got me a nameplate. How thoughtful. When I took my seat the other members of the board came and took their seats, the cameras that were live-streaming the meeting got into position, and the crowd that had come to hear the fate of the company took their seats.

I leaned into the mic and said, "Members of the board, audience, and those of you at home, thank you for joining us this afternoon. Let us begin."

I slowly rose from my chair and passed out a copy of my paper to each of the board members. They looked at me with uncertainty because this was highly unusual. But I persisted in my presentation. I stopped to adjust my bowtie and hat before I grabbed the mic and walked down to the few steps to the floor.

"Ladies and gentlemen of the board, what I have laid out in front of you is a very long and detailed paper on my plans for this company as a majority stockholder."

The room was dead silent, not soul dared move or make a noise. Everyone was on the edge of their seats waiting for what I had to say next. I looked in the camera and said, "Instead of taking the time to read all twelve pages, I have decided to give everyone a brief synopsis of the details laid out by this paper. I'll try and put all of this in terms that anyone can understand. Would that be alright with the members of the board?"

All the members shook their heads yes. So, I proceeded.

"It's very clear that this company is on a downward spiral," I said walking around the front taking turns looking at the board members, audience and the cameras, "Over the past two months I have been putting together a plan to get things back on track. I arrived at two solutions and I'll go ahead and spell each of those out for you."

I took a deep breath, "Our first solution requires nothing on the part of the other board members. I will start by relieving the current CEO of Brumfield trailers of his position and instate myself as CEO."

I was interrupted by the CEO of Brumfield Trailers who was on the board, "You can't do that."

I whipped around and stared him down, "Watch me. As a majority stockholder, I have the power to do whatever I please. Now sit your ass down and let me finish."

He sat down defeated and I continued, "After letting go of the current CEO, I will then begin to rid this company of the massive debt that has accrued over the past few years. I will start by firing every fucking employee, I will sell every scrap of aluminum in that warehouse to Ford Motor Company for pennies on the dollar, I will then sell every welder, drill, and screw until we have a blank slate. Next, I will enter negotiations to try and get us out of this mess where I will try and get us a better deal on aluminum and secure us new sound contracts. I will tear this company limb from limb until we can get back on our feet."

Everyone in the room had wide and gaping mouths. They were all aghast with every word that just came out of my mouth. I smiled.

"Or we have one other option. This option also requires no extra effort from anyone on the board. I propose Brumfield Trailers merge with Starlight Trailers and let them assume management."

The room buzzed. All the board members looked back and forth at each and talked. Finally, one of the members who I believe is related to Rucker Davis in some way got everyone to quiet down before she spoke into her mic, "We do not want to merge with Starlight Trailers, our founders wouldn't have wanted that."

I turned to look at her, "Nobody wants to merge with us, we have a three to one debt ratio, it would be easier to sell typewriters. The fact is, Starlight trailers have cheap aluminum contracts that are locked down."

"So, what if we don't like either of those options?" Another board member said.

"That sucks because right now those are our only two options." I paused and looked out at the audience, "Before we leave here today, the board members will vote on which option they prefer, and I will respect the outcome and join the side with the most votes."

The discussion raged on for an hour longer. Which was understandable, nobody was going to like either outcome. At this point for them, it was picking the lesser of two evils. Deep down I knew that almost every person in this room loathed me. I was praying that at least one soul had the smarts to figure out that I was saving this company. In business and in life you have to make tough decisions, that's a given. You cannot let emotion cloud your judgment or else you try too hard to please every party. I do understand that it is hypocritical of me to say such things when the driving force behind this company takeover was solely revenge. But if you examine further, the motive behind the company merger was purely a strategical business move on my part.

"Let's hold it to a vote," I said.

The board members hesitated but every single member unanimously voted to merge. And with that, our first board meeting was finished. Today wasn't just a victory for me but a victory for this company and my families. After everyone cleared out I gathered my things and walked out of the meeting room. The road ahead of me was going to be long, merging companies isn't going to be easy for anyone but I'm willing to make it work.

I clicked the button on the elevator and waited for the door to open. Once inside the clicked the button for the first floor, the little yellow light flickered on and the door shut. I pulled out my phone and texted Kaitlyn to let her know the meeting was over. The metal on the door reflected my image. I saw myself, in a suit and cowboy hat. The elevator played the somber tune of Uncle Lucius entitled, *Keep the Wolves Away*.

Finally, I felt the elevator slowing down. When the elevator stopped the doors didn't open at first. I just sat there in a non-moving elevator. Suddenly, I heard the ding that signaled my arrival on the first floor. The doors slowly opened to reveal a man standing in front of the entrance. Deep down I knew I had lived this before. I watched the man stare at me. I memorized his facial features, and I recognized him. During the meeting, he sat at the back and just stared, with an expressionless face. After a while, he raised his right hand and put it across his body into his jacket. My heart sank to my stomach. Time passed in slow motion. He pulled a handgun out of his jacket at the pace of a snail and aimed the barrel at my chest.

I was losing time and soon I was about to lose my life if I didn't do anything. I reached out my arms, ducked my left shoulder. I grabbed the middle part of the gun and pulled the gun towards my body as I rolled to the left, avoiding the barrel. He fired the gun. The cold steel turned flaming hot to the touch as the bullet traveled from the tip of the barrel to the wall of the elevator. On impact, the bullet splintered the wood panel.

With both hands still on the gun, I then took my left hand off and rammed my elbow as hard I possibly could in the man's eye. Instinctively he howled in pain and backed up in the hallway. Without a second to waste, I lunged at him with a closed fist and landed a single blow to his nose. Blood began to pour from his nostrils. However, he regained his balance quickly and rammed the butt of the gun down on my forehead. I felt light-headed and a trickle of blood ran down my forehead. The fire of rage burned inside me. I landed two more blows on the assassin. The first blow landed in his ribs, I could feel the cracking of bone as I made contact, the second landed on his collar bone. He dropped the gun out of pain, and I kicked it down the hallway.

The man shoved my chest and I backed up a few feet stunned from the previous blow to my head. We both locked eyes as we took long deep breaths. I looked over to see where the gun was and back at the man. The gun wasn't too far but still a measurable distance. I turned and sprinted for it. From somewhere behind me I heard the man pick up a tall metal trash can. Before I knew it, the metal can hit me in the back and from the force of the throw, it knocked me to the ground. As I fell I turned to see the man just standing there staring. When I made impact, my head took a majority of the force. My vision became clouded and my body movements were lethargic.

I slowly looked in front of me and the gun was just inches from my face. I started to move my arms to grab it, they moved slowly, and the man was approaching from behind. My bloody fingertips touched the cold steel and made their way down to the smooth, rubber gripped handle. I clutched the gun and rolled over to see the man almost standing over me. I raised the gun. My clouded vision and now pounding headache made aiming a tough feat. I fired two rounds. The two shell casings exited the gun and bounced off arm, leaving my skin burning. The man collapsed on the floor next to me.

We both lied on the floor. I could see the man choking on his own blood as a small pool formed around his mouth.

"Who…are…you…" I struggled to say.

Every word he choked on a little more blood, "Actions… have… consequences…" he coughed and sprayed blood on the floor in front of him,
"You're…dancing…with…the… devil…now"

The air around me became quite cold, and the light became harsh and blinding. I could feel my eyes roll into the back of my head. Darkness.

Chapter 12

My mind just kept replaying the scene over and over again. The fight, the words he spoke, the fuzzy memories of the blue and red flashing lights. It's quite the awful dream to keep having. I thought that the reason I was still stuck in the hospital was because of a concussion. But it turns out that sometime during that fight the scab that had formed after my pituitary gland surgery had busted and was leaking blood. Fun. For the past two days, I have done a lot more sleeping than anything and it bothered me because I couldn't do anything else.

The bland hospital room was decorated with a mounted television from the age of dinosaurs, and a small framed picture on the wall of a single flower. Kaitlyn was passed out in a large chair across from me. She was snoring softly. I felt bad for being hurt because it meant our lives would be upside down for a while and Kaitlyn would have to adapt. Lexi was curled up next to me on the very large hospital bed. My whole family right in front of me. It still made my heart swell to know that I finally had a family. Kaitlyn had asked me the other night if Lexi would ever call her mom. I told her I couldn't say for sure, but whatever it is she decides to call us, we will be happy either way.

The nurse came in to check on me every two hours. When she came in she always woke Lexi up and shooed her out of the bed. This time when she came in, she let Lexi stay.

She ran my vitals and drew some blood and left me alone. About an hour later Kaitlyn wanted to go get me dinner and I let her. I also asked her to bring me my laptop so I could work on something and keep what little sanity I had left. Whenever they left I fell asleep again.

I was awakened suddenly but the sound of the door shutting. Whenever I opened my eyes I was shocked to find a tall man standing at the end of my bed. I studied him up and down. The man had on a black suit with a black cowboy hat and bolo tie with a large turquoise piece in the middle of an even large metal piece. The man had extremely pale skin and when I looked closer, he had two different colored eyes, one was extremely blue, and the other was brown.

"Who are you?" I asked groggily.

"You don't need to worry about that right now," he said, "It's good to see you're doing well."

"Did you have something to do with my attack?" I asked, trying to sit up in bed.

"When I first heard about you, I thought you were some big-headed, insignificant prick, but I will admit I was wrong, you're a lot stronger than I had originally anticipated. That's why this is going to be so much more fun."

The man finished talking and walked towards the door as I sputtered more questions. I still felt weak, but I tried to climb out of bed to follow the man out. However, as soon as I tried to balance myself, I got extremely lightheaded and crumpled to the floor.

He stood in the doorway and stared down at me as I looked up at him. I struggled as I tried to pull myself off the floor.

"If I were you, I'd get ready for a fight. You can bet your ass a war is coming between you and me." And with those final words, he was gone.

The End

Of Part I